©Carole Marsh/Gallopade International/Peachtree City, GA
©2010 Paperback ISBN: 978-0-635-07505-5
©2010 Library Binding ISBN: 978-0-635-07549-9

Gallopade is proud to be a member of these educational organizations and associations:

American Library Association (ALA)
The National School Supply and Equipment Association (NSSEA)
The National Council for the Social Studies (NCSS)
National Association for Gifted Children (NAGC)
American Booksellers Association (ABA)
Museum Store Association (MSA)
International Reading Association (IRA)
Supporter of **Association of Partners for Public Lands (APPL)**

Published by
GALLOPADE INTERNATIONAL
800-536-2GET
www.gallopade.com

CAROLE MARSH BOOKS

Other Carole Marsh Books

Orville & Wilbur Wright . . . Step Out Into The Sky!
Lewis & Clark Go On a Hike: The Story of the Corps of Discovery
The Louisiana Purchase: "What A Deal!"
The American Revolution: How Our Nation Was Born
The American Civil War: When Brother Fought Brother
The U.S. Civil Rights Movement: The Fight For Equality
The Bill of Rights: "It Can't Be Wrong!"
U.S. Constitution: "Sign on the Dotted Line!"
The Declaration of Independence: "Quit Bossing Us Around!"
Jamestown: America's First Permanent English Settlement
The Underground Railroad: Path to Freedom
Industrial Revolution: From Muscles to Machines!
Great Depression & the New Deal: Brother, Can You Spare a Dime?
World War II: When Men, Women, and Children Saved the World
Brown v. Board of Education: I Want to Go to School!
World War I: The War to End All Wars!
Abraham Lincoln: America's 16th President
The U.S. Supreme Court: The Keepers of the Laws of Our Land
Galloping West with the Pony Express!: "The Mail Must Go Through!"
The Transcontinental Railroad: The Big Race to the Golden Spike!
The 13 Colonies: A New Life in a New World!
Wagons Ho! Pioneers' Path to the West!: The Oregon Trail

State Stuff™, Available for all 50 states:

My First Pocket Guide
State My First Book
State Wheel of Fortune Gamebook
State Survivor Gamebook
State Illustrated Timelines
"Jography!": A Fun Run Through Our State
The State Coloring Book
The Big Reproducible Activity Book
State Millionaire Gamebook
State Project Books
Jeopardy: Answers & Questions About Our State

Patriotic Favorites™

Patriotic Favorites Coloring Book
Patriotic Biographies
The Daily Patriot: 365 Quotations
Young Patriots Coloring & Activity Book
Patriotic Projects
Patriotisms: 365 Definitions

Table of Contents

A Word from the Author

Dear Reader,

How I love the Old West! And how surprised I was to learn that the Pony Express—a true icon of that period in history—only lasted for about 18 months! It was such a daring idea—to launch riders and horses in a continual relay from Missouri to California to deliver the mail across plains and rivers and mountains and deserts. What a logistics nightmare! But whatever the challenges, this growing nation was determined to tackle them!

Who were these riders? Who were the risk-taking entrepreneurs who undertook this challenge? Who were the station keepers who manned the lonely outposts along the way? How did the horses survive the demands made on them? How did riders persevere through rain and snow, summer and winter? What caused the end of the Pony Express?

We worked very hard at researching this book, but did find some myth mixed with fact, and conflicting information. I have learned that many of the Pony Express company records were lost and the history of this time period wasn't truly documented until the early 20th century.

You'll find lots of fascinating information in this book. And you'll also find life lessons for your students—like daring to dream, the power of ingenuity, persevering against setbacks and obstacles, and how new technologies affect change in every generation. I hope you enjoy this ride on the Pony Express! If we pay attention and learn from it, history is a wonderful teacher!

Giddy Up!

Carole Marsh

A Timeline of Events

1841	First organized wagon train heads west over the Rocky Mountains.
January 24, 1848	James Marshall discovers gold in California.
August 19, 1848	New York Herald prints news of the gold discovery, and the California Gold Rush follows.
September 9, 1850	California becomes 31st state.
September 15, 1858	Butterfield Overland Mail begins stagecoach mail service from St. Louis to San Francisco. The trip takes 25 days.
October 1859	Central Overland California and Pikes Peak Express Company (the official name for the Pony Express) is established.
April 3, 1860	Pony Express is launched with riders leaving St. Joseph, Missouri and Sacramento, California simultaneously. Their goal is to deliver the mail in 10 days.
October 24, 1861	Transcontinental telegraph is completed, marking the end of the Pony Express.
May 10, 1869	Transcontinental railroad is completed at Promontory Summit, Utah.

Galloping West with the Pony Express:

"The Mail Must Go Through!"

The story of the Pony Express is one of the most fascinating tales of the Old West! Simply put, the Pony Express was a fast-moving relay system where riders and horses carried the mail from Missouri to California.

It took bold young horsemen. It took sturdy, swift ponies. It took dedicated station masters at lonely outposts. It took determination and endurance. It demanded the bravest of men and the strongest of horses to complete the exhausting journey.

Each mail carrier made his way alone. He rode across plains, mountains, and deserts. A fresh horse awaited him at stations along the way. A new rider was poised at his last station, ready to seize the mail and gallop out of sight. There was no time to lose! The mail must go through!

You've Got Mail—or Not!

The United States grew quickly in the mid-1800s. Thousands of pioneers began moving west on the Oregon Trail. The number of people in California exploded due to the Gold Rush in 1849.

How did these new residents of the West get their mail? Very slowly! In 1845, President James Polk sent a message to California from Washington, D.C. It took six months to arrive. Mail to the West traveled by ship at that time. Once a ship reached Panama, workers carried the mail across the isthmus and loaded it onto another ship for the rest of the journey. That had to change!

Overland mail services tried to improve mail delivery in the late 1850s. But it still took almost a month to get mail across the country. When gold was found at Pikes Peak in Colorado in 1858, the cry for quicker mail service grew louder. Growing businesses needed to communicate faster!

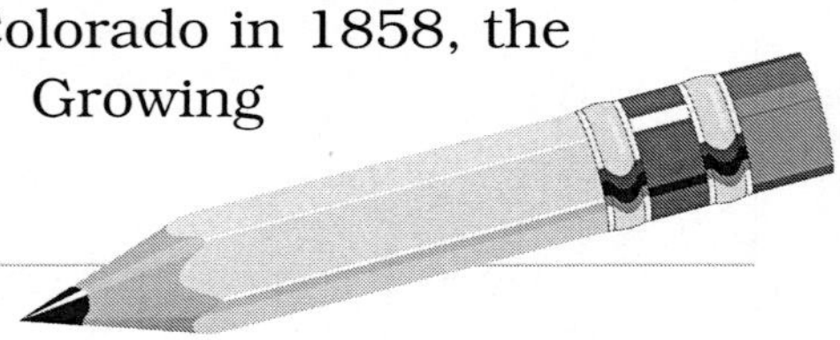

Complete the time line!

Look at the time line below. On each line, write the events listed below in the correct order.

Pioneers move west on Oregon Trail
Gold found at Pikes Peak
Mail took a month to get across U.S.
California Gold Rush
Polk's message took six months by mail

mid-1800s | 1845 | 1849 | late 1850s | 1858

Who Started It?

Three partners launched the Pony Express in late 1859. Their names were William Russell, Alexander Majors, and William Waddell. The three men had experience moving freight around the United States. They named their new business the Central Overland California and Pikes Peak Express Company. Its nickname became the "Pony Express"!

The partners decided to start the Pony Express operation in the spring of 1860. They had a lot to do in a few short months! They had to hire riders and station masters. They had to buy 400 to 500 quality horses. They had to set up more than 100 stations along the route. They had to organize central offices to handle the mail. They had to buy supplies like hay, horseshoes, and flour. And finally, they had to send the supplies to remote stations. That was not an easy task in those days!

Have You Got What It Takes?

Circle the words that play an important role in achieving success.

EXCUSES

PATIENCE

COMPLAINING

TIME

LAZINESS

WHINING

OPTIMISM

DETERMINATION

BRAINSTORMING

GIVING UP

ORGANIZATION

COOPERATION

How It Worked

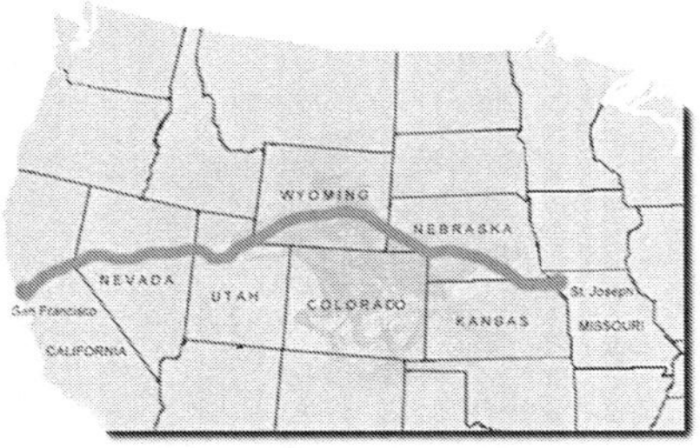

The Pony Express ran in two directions. The westbound route started in St. Joseph, Missouri and ended in San Francisco, California. The eastbound route ran from San Francisco to St. Joseph. The goal was to make the journey in 10 days—over 1,996 miles!

Each rider rode between 75 and 100 miles. They changed horses at relay stations about every 10 to 15 miles. Horses traveled about 10 miles per hour. A one-way trip required 75 horses. At relay stations, riders took their mailbag and jumped on a fresh horse. When a rider reached his last station, a new rider grabbed the mailbag and took off in a cloud of dust!

The Pony Express route ran through parts of eight states. St. Joseph was the starting point because it was the last town served by the railroad coming from eastern cities. The railroad brought the mail to St. Joseph for delivery by the Pony Express.

Where Did They Ride?

Study the map of the Pony Express route below. List the states that Pony Express riders traveled through.

1. ______________________
2. ______________________
3. ______________________
4. ______________________
5. ______________________
6. ______________________
7. ______________________
8. ______________________

Really Ready Riders!

WANTED

Young, skinny, wiry fellows not over 18.
Must be expert riders willing to risk death daily.
Orphans preferred.

William Russell ran newspaper ads for Pony Express riders. He initially hired 80 riders. Almost all of them weighed less than 125 pounds. They were paid $50 per month. They also got a free place to stay and free food.

Each rider took the oath of the Pony Express. They agreed not to get drunk or use bad language. They also agreed not to fight with other Pony Express employees. Each rider received a leather-bound Bible. They also carried weapons including two revolvers, a knife, and a lightweight rifle.

Some reports say the youngest Pony Express rider was just 13 years old! But whatever the age, a rider had to be tough. Accidents, falls, and terrible weather conditions faced them along the trail. But they were brave! They were also well aware of how important their job was to their growing country!

Make a Neckerchief!

Pony Express riders often wore neckerchiefs to protect their nose and mouth from dust and strong winds. Follow the directions to make one of your own.

1. Fold a bandana in half to form a triangle. If you don't have a bandana, you can use leftover lightweight fabric cut to a size of about 16 inches square.

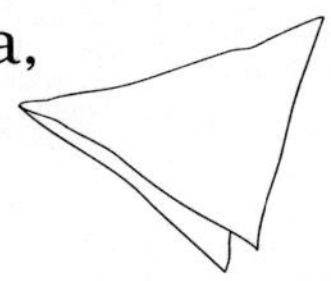

2. Tie the ends in an overhand knot.

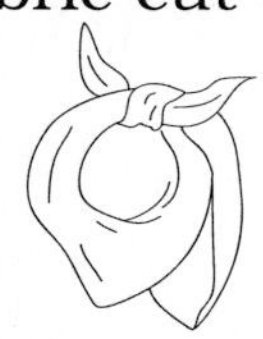

3. Tie a second overhand knot going the other direction. If your knot looks square, you have tied a square knot like the cowboys used. (If it doesn't look square, you have tied a double knot, which won't hold as well.)

4. Wear your neckerchief with the knot in the back. Be ready to pull it over your mouth when the dust blows!

Prime Ponies

The Pony Express owners did not try to save money when buying horses. They needed strong, reliable horses and were willing to pay top dollar to get them. The cost of horses was about $200 per horse. That was a high price at the time.

Different types of horses were needed for different parts of the country. Small, sure-footed mountain ponies were best for mountainous areas. Riders on the Great Plains had bigger, faster horses. Mormons in the West rounded up wild mustangs and sold them to the Pony Express. Almost all of the horses were mares. They were more reliable than stallions.

Horses did not have an easy time on the Pony Express. Many had to run further than planned due to weather or an Indian attack. Some stepped in prairie dog burrows and threw their riders. Several even died after being worked too hard. Others were stolen by Indians.

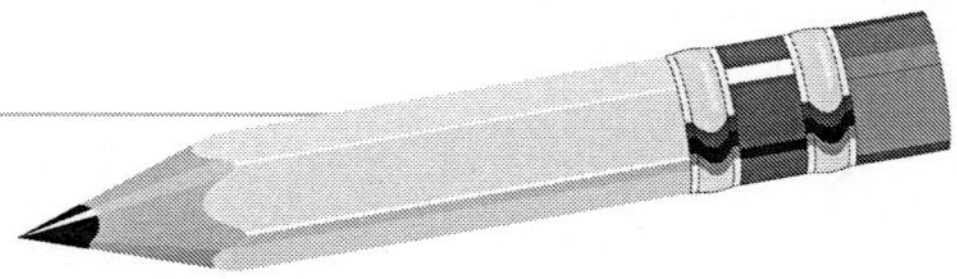

Do the Math!

Answer the following math questions related to the Pony Express.

1 Missouri Mike traveled 85 miles on his Pony Express route. How many horses did he need if each horse ran 15 miles except for one that ran 10 miles? __________

2 Nevada Ned sold 12 horses to the Pony Express. He got a check for $2,340. How much did each horse sell for?

____

3 Bronco Bill and his horse traveled 35 miles at 10 miles per hour. How many hours did it take them? __________ How many minutes? __________

4 The ponies at Fort Kearny needed all of their shoes replaced. If Blacksmith Bob used 24 horseshoes in one day, how many horses did he shoe? __________ If he had 92 shoes in his shop, how many did he have left?

____

Mind Your Mailbag!

Pony Express mail was carried in a special carrier. It was called a mochila, the Spanish word for knapsack. This single piece of leather lay over the saddle. It had four pockets called cantinas which held the mail. Three of the pockets were locked. The fourth was open for mail that was to be picked up or delivered along the route.

The mochila had a hole for the saddle horn and a split for the cantle. Since it was not attached to the saddle, it could be removed quickly when the rider changed horses. The rider sat on it with his legs between the rear and front pockets. A mochila could carry from 12 to 15 pounds of mail.

The mail itself was wrapped in oiled cloth to protect it from rain, snow, and sweat from the horses. The original postage on the Pony Express was $5.00 per half-ounce. That was very expensive! (In those days, $1.00 per day was considered good pay!) The cost of mail was later reduced to $1.00 per half-ounce.

What Do You Know?

Use the word bank to fill in the blanks below.

Word Bank		
leather	sweat	mochila
saddle	knapsack	oiled
cantinas	expensive	postage

1. Pony Express mail was carried in a bag called a ______________________________, the Spanish word for ______________________________.
2. This mailbag was made of ______________________________.
3. Pockets that held the mail were called ______________________________.
4. Mail was wrapped in ______________________ cloth to protect it from rain, snow, and ______________________________ from horses.
5. A hole in the mailbag fit over the ______________________________ horn.
6. The original ______________________________ on the Pony Express was ______________________________.

Meet Pony Bob

One of the most famous riders on the Pony Express was "Pony Bob" Haslam. He was part of the fastest trip on the Pony Express—7 days and 17 hours. The mailbag contained President Lincoln's Inaugural Address!

Pony Bob also made the longest round trip on the Pony Express. It happened in present-day Nevada. When Bob reached his relief station, the new rider refused to take the mail. He was afraid of Indians on the route ahead. Bob kept riding for a total distance of 190 miles. He rested for nine hours, then headed back west. He ended up riding 380 miles round trip!

Write an Article!

Write a newspaper article to describe one of Pony Bob's historic rides! Make up your own details to bring the story to life!

1. Masthead (Name of newspaper-make one up!)
2. Date Happened (Write on this line.)
3. Dateline (Place where happened)
4. BIG HEADLINE!
5. Tell the news!
6. Photo (Draw a picture.)
7. Sidebar (Put a quotation or trivia fact in lower right box.)
8. Editor (Hey, that's you!)

Did you know!...

Editor:

Staying at the Station

The Pony Express route was divided into five divisions from east to west. There were two types of stations—home and relay. Riders stayed overnight at home stations and changed horses at relay stations. Home stations were from 65 to 100 miles apart. Relay stations (or swing stations) were 10 to 15 miles apart. The distance depended on the difficulty of the terrain.

Home stations had a station keeper and several helpers. Sometimes the keeper's wife and family lived there, too. At the home station, riders would find fresh ponies, a bunk to sleep in, food, and a blacksmith shop. Home stations often hosted passengers traveling on the Overland Stagecoach.

Relay stations were much smaller. Often they consisted of a shack near a source of water. They were manned by one or two men. Riders exchanged horses at relay stations. Both types of stations were located in remote areas. The main excitement came once or twice a week when a rider arrived!

Blacksmiths at home stations were critical to the success of the Pony Express! Horses often lost shoes on their wild rides!

Meet Your Match!

Match the pictures with the correct station—home or relay. Write H for home station, and R for relay station.

1. 

2. 

3. 

4. 

5. 

6. 

7. 

Not an Easy Life

The Pony Express tried to use existing ranches as stations whenever possible. But many isolated posts had to be set up along the mail route. The life of a station keeper in these places was not an easy one. Temperatures soared in the summer and plunged in the winter. Storms were also a threat. Indian attacks were a constant concern. And the food was often just plain awful!

So who wanted to live in these remote locations? The jobs were sometimes taken by people running from the law. Other station keepers were people who just didn't fit into normal society.

No matter what their reason for living at a station, these keepers had to be smart. Nevada station keeper Jay Kelley had to take over for a rider who was wounded by Indians. Mary Faylor, wife of a rider, fooled some Indians snooping around a station. She stuck hats and caps on sticks and put them near the windows. The Indians thought that men were inside when Mary was actually alone!

Write About It!

Pretend you are Mary Faylor. Write a journal entry about your narrow escape.

Date: ______________

Name: ______________________________

____

____

____

____

____

____

____

____

Legends and Lore

Much of Pony Express history has been mixed with myth over the years. Is it real? Is it not? Here are a few examples:

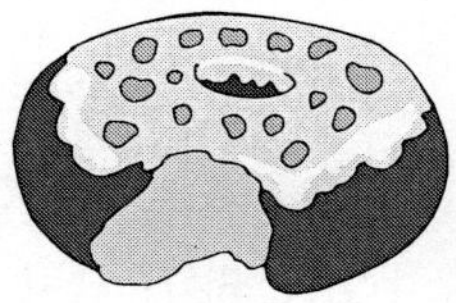

Many say that the donut was born on the Pony Express! The story says that the Dooley girls of Troy, Kansas liked to bake pastries for a rider named Johnny Frye. But as he rode by, he had trouble grabbing the pastries with one hand. To solve the problem, the girls put a hole in the center of the pastry. That way Johnny could hook it with one finger!

Was William F. Cody, or "Buffalo Bill," really a rider on the Pony Express? He would have been just 15 years old. He says he was, but some historians doubt his claim. What is known is that Buffalo Bill had worked for the owners of the Pony Express driving cattle prior to the mail service. So maybe they did hire the young man! No one knows for sure.

Buffalo Bill earned his nickname for his skill as a buffalo hunter in the late 1860s.

Make Your Own Donuts!

Follow the directions below to make delicious donuts.

Ingredients:
1 can of biscuit dough
¼ to ½ c cooking oil; vegetable or canola
cinnamon and sugar mixture

You will also need a frying pan, a pair of tongs, a sheet of wax paper, some paper towels, and a small cap from a bottle to use as a hole cutter.

Directions:
Open the biscuit can and spread them out on a sheet of wax paper. Use the cap to press out a donut hole in the center of each biscuit. Add oil to a frying pan. Bring oil to a medium heat. You'll need enough oil to cover half of the donut when cooking. Place a few donuts into the pan and let cook until golden brown. They cook quickly! Turn them over and brown the other side. Use tongs to remove donuts and then put them on the paper towels to drain and cool slightly. Sprinkle the cinnamon sugar mixture on the donuts while they are warm. Don't forget to cook the holes, too!

Was the Mail Ever Lost?

Information from the St. Joseph Museum says that mail was lost twice on the Pony Express. However, only one complete mailbag was lost.

The first incident occurred in May 1860. The mail arrived a day late in St. Joseph. When it arrived, it had mail from Salt Lake City, but not California. A note from Salt Lake City was attached to the waybill. The note was published in the New York Daily Tribune: "The rider has just come in. The Indians have chased all the men from the stations between Diamond Spring and Carson Valley. The pouch in which the express matter is carried is lost."

The second incident happened in August 1860. A horse arrived at Carson River, Nevada without a rider or mailbag. No one knows what happened!

Make the Pony Express Come Alive!

Follow the directions below to make a Pony Express landscape.

Materials: Watercolor paint and brush, white drawing paper, water, black construction paper (alternative: black paint or black crayon)

Directions:

1. Paint the white paper in horizontal stripes painting blue at the top, then purple, then red, then orange, then yellow at the bottom. Blend the area between each stripe so the colors are not hard stripes. Allow the paint to dry.

2. Draw an outline of a Pony Express rider on the black paper. Leave an inch of black along the bottom. Cut it out and glue to the yellow area on the painted paper. (This figure can also be drawn on the white paper first so that a light line can be seen after the paint is applied. The figure can then be painted in with black paint or black crayon.)

You have created a colorful Pony Express landscape!

The Biggest Fear

Pony Express riders feared Indian attacks. The worst problems were in Nevada and Utah. The first trouble began in May 1860. Pony Express stations were often set up near sources of water. Water was a scarce resource. Nearby Indians became angry. They drove the horses off from the Roberts Creek station. Next, they burned the Williams station. They were fighting back after an attack by the white men.

These skirmishes set off a number of Indian attacks. These raids interrupted the Pony Express schedule. They also caused death and destruction. Seven relay stations were destroyed, 16 employees were killed, and 150 horses were driven away. The Pony Express owners lost about $75,000 worth of equipment and horses. Finally, government troops were able to stop the trouble by the end of June.

Spell It Out!

It was devastating to the Pony Express when horses were lost during Indian attacks. Using the letters below, write an acrostic poem about the horses in the Pony Express. One item has been completed for you.

H

O

R

S

Excellent quality

Aggravated by Animals!

Wild animals often caused problems for Pony Express riders. Experts say that more than 40 million buffalo roamed the Great Plains at that time! Massive herds blocked the trail from time to time. Pioneers estimated that some of the herds had one million buffalo in them! Riders had to be careful not to startle them and cause a stampede.

Buffalo wallows posed a danger as well. These were low areas where herds had worn away the soil by rolling in the dust. A rider named William Campbell was thrown from his horse after it stepped in a wallow. The horse ran back to the last station. Luckily, the mailbag fell off too. William grabbed it and got a ride from a passing stagecoach!

Hungry wolves sometimes followed the riders. William Campbell told another story of coming upon a pack of wolves eating a buffalo carcass. The wolves started to chase him, but his horse outran them. He decided to poison the next buffalo carcass he saw. When he came back to it, he saw 12 dead wolves!

True or False?

Read the statements below. Write T for True and F for False.

____ 1. Wild animals caused problems for Pony Express riders.

____ 2. About six million buffalo roamed the Great Plains while the Pony Express was in operation.

____ 3. Buffalo quickly moved out of the way when a Pony Express rider appeared on the trail.

____ 4. A buffalo wallow is a small lake where buffalo herds gathered to drink.

____ 5. William Campbell lost his mailbag when his horse threw him.

____ 6. Hungry wolves followed riders from time to time.

____ 7. William Campbell killed a group of wolves by poisoning a buffalo carcass.

"The greatest danger I faced on the trail was buffaloes. If a rider ran into a herd, he was gone."
-William Campbell

Weather Woes

The Pony Express was often able to meet their 10-day delivery goal in summer. But winter was another story. The ride could take from 12 to 16 days.

Heavy snow caused big problems. Riders often got through by following mule trains. Even then, riding the trail was dangerous. If a horse stepped off the trail, he could easily plunge into snow up to his belly. Riders risked getting lost in blinding snowstorms. One night, a rider named Billy Fisher got caught in a blizzard. He said he was so cold he was tempted to start a fire by burning some of the U.S. mail! Billy finally came across a remote cabin in the woods. He stumbled in and was cared for by an old man until morning.

Summer and spring had their own share of weather woes. Violent thunderstorms could quickly turn flat land into mud pits. In spring, rivers swelled with icy water from the mountains. Riders and horses risked their lives crossing them. Insects caused problems, too. Clouds of mosquitoes pestered them and mobs of grasshoppers sometimes blocked their path!

Pony Express Puzzle!

Use the clues below to complete the crossword puzzle.

Word Bank

summer	winter	snow
thunderstorm	rivers	mosquito

Clues:

Across

5. Lightning usually occurs during this

Down

1. Biting insect
2. Blinding snowstorms could occur during this season
3. Icy, rushing water in these was dangerous to riders and horses
4. Hottest season of the year
6. Caused big problems in the winter

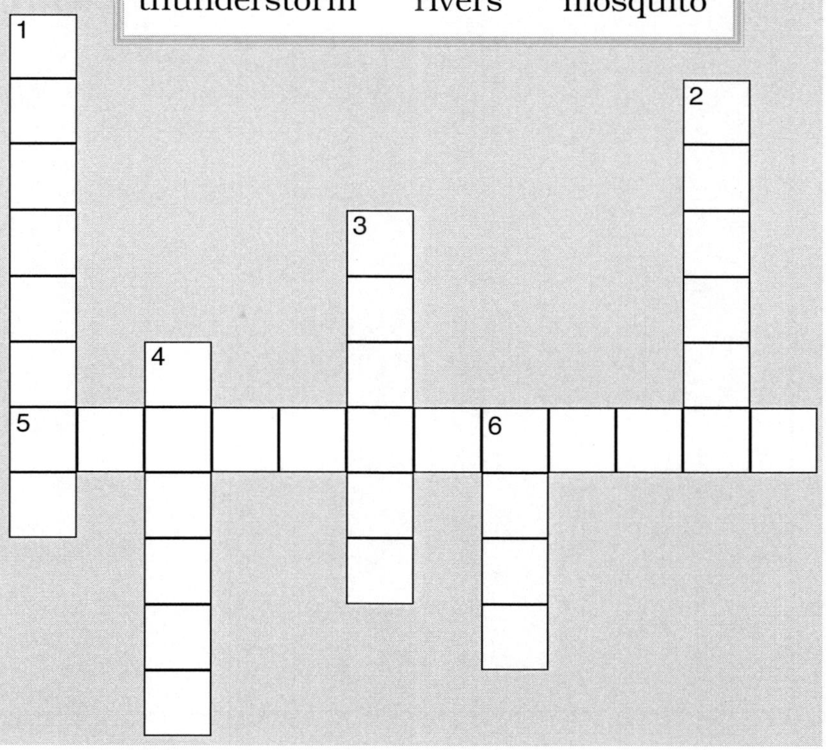

The End of the Line

The Pony Express route officially ended in San Francisco, California. However, Sacramento was the end of the line for most riders. They usually rode up to the docks on the Sacramento River. The steamship *Antelope* waited there to take the mail to San Francisco. The rider passed the mochila to the ship's captain.

If a rider missed the *Antelope*, he had to ride on through three more stations before reaching the true "end of the line." The Pony Express officially ended at 153 Montgomery Street in San Francisco.

How did people in San Francisco know they had mail? The local newspaper posted an announcement and listed the names on the letters. Citizens hurried to the Pony Express office to pick up their mail. Hey—you've got mail!

Great News!

Create a newspaper announcement to tell citizens that the mail has arrived! Make it eye-catching so it stands out in the paper. Be sure to list the names of those who have letters waiting!

Telegraph Takeover

The Pony Express ended when the transcontinental telegraph was completed in October 1861. Now, important news could be sent instantly over wires!

Even though the telegraph offered quick communication, many Californians still longed for the Pony Express. The telegraph had a few problems getting started. Sometimes buffalo leaned on telegraph posts and knocked them over. Indians sometimes threw blankets over the wires and yanked them to the ground.

But it was too late. The bill Congress had passed giving the go-ahead for the telegraph stated that the Pony Express would end when the telegraph was completed. The "talking wires," as the Indians called them, spelled the end to this amazing undertaking. Simply put, the Pony Express is one of the finest examples of creativity, determination, and the will to succeed in American history!

End of an Era

Answer the questions below about the Pony Express.

1. When was the transcontinental telegraph completed? ____________________

2. What are some reasons that Californians wanted the Pony Express to continue operating?

   ____

   ____

   ____

3. What governmental body said that the Pony Express would end when the telegraph was completed?

   ____

4. Explain why you think the Pony Express is a great example of American inventiveness.

   ____

   ____

   ____

   ____

Pony Express—The End?!

What was this telegraph that spelled the end for the Pony Express? The telegraph sent electronic signals along iron wires. It used a code system invented by Samuel Morse called "Morse code." Dots and dashes stand for letters in Morse code. The telegraph printed the dots and dashes on pieces of paper.

In 1843, the U.S. Congress gave Morse money to build a telegraph line from Washington, D.C. to Baltimore, Maryland. They wanted to see if it would work! Morse sent his first successful Morse code message in 1844. Soon, telegraph lines appeared along railroad tracks. They helped railroad operators communicate and keep trains running safely and on time. The telegraph also spread news around the country in minutes. That was never possible before!

All rapid long-distance communication depended on the telegraph until the late 1870s. What changed then? The telephone was invented and changed communication forever!

Dash, Dash, Dot, Dot

Morse code uses dashes and dots to communicate. Use the code below to find out the motto of the Pony Express.

A	B	C	D	E	F	G	H	I
•▬	▬•••	▬•▬•	▬••	•	••▬•	▬▬•	••••	••

J	K	L	M	N	O	P	Q	R
•▬▬▬	▬•▬	•▬••	▬▬	▬•	▬▬▬	•▬▬•	▬▬•▬	•▬•

S	T	U	V	W	X	Y	Z
•••	▬	••▬	•••▬	•▬▬	▬••▬	▬•▬▬	▬▬••

___ ___ ___ ___ ___ ___ ___ ___ ___ ___ ___

▬ •••• • ▬▬ •▬ •• •▬•• ▬▬ ••▬ ••• ▬

___ ___ ___ ___ ___ ___ ___ ___ ___

▬▬• ▬▬▬ ▬ •••• •▬• ▬▬▬ ••▬ ▬▬• ••••

Happy Anniversary!

The Pony Express may have only lasted a short time, but it holds a permanent place in the history of the West. Its riders and horses performed an amazing feat! They delivered almost 35,000 pieces of mail on 308 rides each way for a total distance of 616,000 miles! It also blazed the trail for the transcontinental telegraph and railroad.

The Pony Express celebrates its 150th anniversary in 2010! The National Pony Express Association plans a "Re-Ride" event. It will take place over the Pony Express National Historic Trail from June 6 to 26.

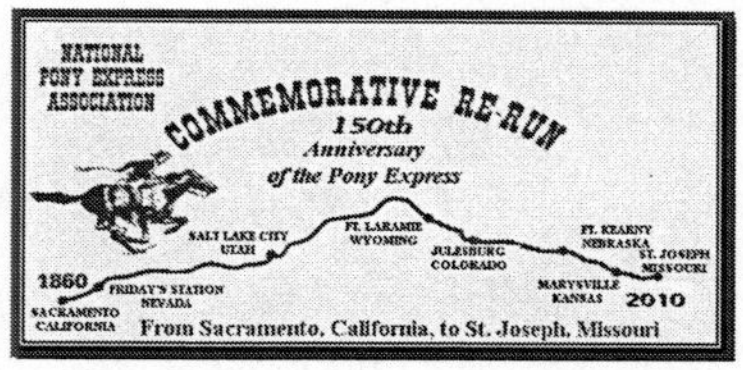

To start the event, mail will be carried by boat from San Francisco to Sacramento. The eight Pony Express states will hold individual celebrations as the riders pass through. Riders will carry commemorative letters in a mochila. The envelopes will have a special U.S. Postal Service cancellation mark.

And, to keep up with modern technology, each mochila will carry a GPS transmitter. The GPS unit will transmit the rider's location to a satellite. That way, he can be tracked in real time!

Design a Stamp!

Use your imagination to design a stamp for the 150th anniversary of the Pony Express.

Materials:

White drawing paper - 4 ½" x 5 ½"
Ruler
Colored pencils
Hole punch

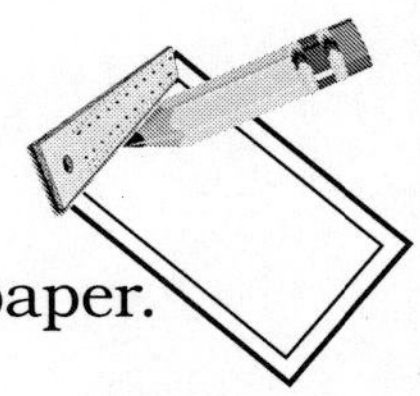

Instructions:

1. Draw a line, using the ruler, about ½" from the outside edge of the paper.
2. Create a design for a stamp within the inside rectangle. Use the Pony Express as your subject. Include the price of the stamp and the letters USA in the design.
3. Color the stamp with colored pencils.
4. Use a hole punch to punch half holes along the outside edge at regular intervals so that the edge appears to be perforated. Your stamp is complete!

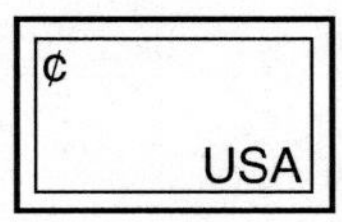

Additional Resources

BOOKS

The Pony Express by Peter Anderson
Wanted—A Few Bold Riders: A Story of the Pony Express by Darice Bailer
Pony Bob's Daring Ride, a Pony Express Adventure by Joe Bensen
Travellers Guide to the Pony Express Trail by Joe Bensen
Pony Express, The Story Behind the Scenery by Anthony Godfrey and Roy Webb
Saddles and Spurs by Raymond W. Settle and Mary Lund Settle

WEBSITES

Pony Express National Historic Trail:
http://www.nps.gov/poex/historyculture/history1.htm

Pony Express Home Station:
http://www.xphomestation.com/frm-faq.html

ASSOCIATIONS

National Pony Express Association, Pollock Pines, CA

HISTORIC SITES AND MUSEUMS:

Pony Express Museum, St. Joseph, MO
Patee House Museum, St. Joseph, MO
Original Pony Express Home Station No. 1 Museum, Marysville, KS
Chimney Rock Station Museum, Bayard, NE
Fort Kearny State Historic Park, Kearney, NE
Harold Warp Pioneer Village, Minder, NE
Wells Fargo History Museum, San Francisco, CA
Folsom Museum, Folsom, CA

Glossary

commemorative: something intended to honor the memory of someone or something

determination: the quality of being strongly motivated to accomplish something

endurance: power to withstand hardship or stress

freight: cargo; goods carried by a large vehicle

ingenuity: ability to solve difficult problems, often in original and creative ways

mare: adult female horse

oath: a solemn promise

outpost: a station located far away from where people live

remote: distant; located far away

stallion: adult male horse used for breeding

stampede: a wild rush of frightened animals

transcontinental: spanning or crossing a continent

Answer Key

Page 8: mid-1800s / Pioneers move west on Oregon Trail; 1845 / Polk's message took six months by mail; 1849 / California Gold Rush; late 1850s / Mail took a month to get across U.S.; 1858 / Gold found at Pikes Peak
Page 9: patience, determination, optimism, brainstorming, cooperation, time, organization
Page 10: Missouri, Kansas, Nebraska, Wyoming, Colorado, Utah, Nevada, California
Page 12: 1. 6; 2. $195; 3. 3.5, 210; 4. 6, 68
Page 13: 1. mochila, knapsack; 2. leather; 3. cantinas; 4. oiled, sweat; 5. saddle; 6. postage, expensive
Page 15: 1. H; 2. R; 3. H; 4. H; 5. R; 6. H; 7. H
Page 20: 1. T; 2. F; 3. F; 4. F; 5. F; 6. T; 7. T
Page 21: Across: 5. thunderstorm; Down: 1. mosquito, 2. winter, 3. rivers, 4. summer, 6. snow
Page 23: 1. October 1861; 2. The telegraph had problems like buffalo knocking over posts or Indians pulling down wires; 3. Congress; 4. Answers will vary
Page 24: The mail must go through!

Index